THE PART-TIME JOB

P. D. James

The Part-Time Job

&

Murder Most Foul

faber

First published in 2020
by Faber & Faber Limited
Bloomsbury House
74–77 Great Russell Street
London WC1B 3DA

'The Part-Time Job' first appeared in the *New Statesman* in 2005
'Murder Most Foul' first appeared in the *Observer* in 1982

Typeset by Faber & Faber Limited
Printed and bound by CPI Group (UK) Ltd, Croydon, CR0 4YY

A CIP record for this book
is available from the British Library

ISBN 978-0-571-36178-6

2 4 6 8 10 9 7 5 3

THE PART-TIME JOB

*B*y the time you read this I shall be dead. Dead for how long, of course, I cannot predict. I shall place this document in the strongroom of my bank with instructions that it shall be sent to the daily newspaper with the largest circulation on the first working day after my funeral. My only regret is that I shan't be alive to savour my retrospective triumph. But that is of small account. I savour it every day of my life. I shall have done the one thing I resolved to do when I was twelve years old – and the world will know it. And the world will be interested, make no mistake about that! I can tell you the precise date when I made up my mind that I would kill Keith Manston-Green. We were both pupils at St Chad's School on the Surrey borders, he the only child of a wealthy businessman with a chain of garages, I from a

3

more humble background, who would never have arrived at St Chad's except for the help of a scholarship endowed by a former pupil and named after him. My six years from eleven to seventeen were years of hell. Keith Manston-Green was the school bully and I was his natural, almost inevitable victim: a scholarship boy, timid, undersized, bespectacled, who never spoke of his parents, was never visited at half-term, wore a uniform that was obviously second-hand and was, like the runt of the litter, destined to be trampled on.

For six years during term time I woke every morning in fear. The masters – some of them at least – must have known what was happening, but it seemed to me they were part of the conspiracy. And Manston-Green was clever. There were never any obvious bruises: the torment was subtler than that.

He was clever in other ways too. Sometimes he would admit me temporarily into his circle of sycophants, give me sweets, share his tuck, stick up for me against the other boys, giving hope to me that all this signalled a change. But there never was a change. There's no point in my reciting the details of his ingenuities. It is enough to say that at six o'clock in the evening on the fifteenth of February 1932, when I was twelve years old, I made a solemn vow: one day I would kill Keith Manston-Green. That vow kept me going for the next five years of torment and remained with me, as strong as when it was first made, through all the years that followed. It may seem odd to you, reading this after my death, that killing Manston-Green should be a lifelong obsession. Surely even childhood cruelty is forgotten at last, or at least put out of mind. But not that cruelty; not my mind. In destroying my childhood, Manston-Green had made me what I am. I knew too that if I forgot that childish oath I would die bitter with regret and self-humiliation. I was in no hurry, but it was something I had to do.

My father had inherited the family business on the fringes of London's East End. He was a locksmith and taught me the trade. The shop was bombed in the war, killing both my parents, but government money compensated for the loss. The house and the shop were rebuilt and I started again. The shop wasn't the only thing I inherited from that secretive, obsessive and unhappy man. I had, like my father had, a part-time job.

Through all the years, I kept track of Keith Manston-Green. I could, of course, have received regular news of him by placing my name on the distribution list for the annual magazine of St Chad's Old Boys' Society, but that seemed to me unwise. I wanted St Chad's to forget I had ever existed. I would rely on my own researches. It wasn't difficult. Manston-Green, like me, had inherited the family business and, motoring through Surrey, I would note every garage I passed which bore his name. I had no difficulty, either, in finding out where he lived. Waiting for my Morris Minor to be filled, I would occasionally say, 'There seems to be quite a number of Manston-Green garages in this part of the world. Is it a private company or something?'

Sometimes the answer would be, 'Search me, guv, haven't a clue.' But other times I got a nugget of information to add to my store. 'Yeah, it's still owned by the family. Keith Manston-Green. Lives outside Stonebridge.' After that it was only a question of consulting the local telephone directory and finding the house.

It was the kind of house I would have expected. A new red-brick monstrosity with gables and mock-Tudor beams, a large garage attached which could take up to four cars, a wide drive and a high privet hedge for privacy, all enclosed in a red-brick wall. A board on the wall said, in mock-antique script, Manston Lodge.

I wasn't in any particular hurry to kill him. What was important was to make sure that the deed was done without suspicion settling on me and, if possible, that the first attempt was successful. It was one of my constant pleasures, scheming over possible methods. But I knew that this mental anticipation could be dangerously self-indulgent. There would come a moment when planning, however satisfying, must give way to action.

When the war broke out in 1939 my fear,

greater than that of the bombing, was that Manston-Green would be killed. The thought that he would die in action and be remembered as a hero was intolerable, but I need not have worried. He joined the RAF, but not as a flier. Those coveted wings were never stitched above the breast pocket of his uniform. He was a Wingless Wonder, as I believe the RAF called them. I think he had something to do with equipment or maintenance and he must have been effective. He ended as a Wing Commander, and naturally he kept the rank in civilian life. His sycophants called him the Wingco – and how he revelled in it.

It was in 1953 that I decided to begin taking active steps towards his elimination. The shop was modestly successful and I had a manager and an assistant, both reliable. My part-time job was an excuse for short absences and I could confidently leave them in charge. I began making short visits to Stonebridge, a prosperous town on the fringes of the commuter belt where my enemy lived. Perhaps the words 'held court' would be more appropriate. He was a member of the local council and of one or two charitable trusts, the kind that confer prestige rather than making unwelcome financial demands, and he was captain of the golf club. Oh yes indeed, he was the 'Wingco', strutting about the clubhouse as he must once have strutted in the Mess.

By then I had discovered quite a lot about Keith Manston-Green. He had divorced his wife, who had left him, taking their two children, and he was now married to Shirley May, twelve years his junior. But it was his captaincy of the Stonebridge Golf Club that gave me an idea how I could get close to him.

I could tell within five minutes of entering the clubhouse that the place reeked of petty suburban snobbery. They didn't actually say what prospective members would be welcome, but I could tell that there was a set of clearly understood conventions designed to enable the members to feel superior to all but the chosen few, most of them successful local businessmen. However, they were as keen on increasing their income as were less snobbish enterprises and it was possible to pay green fees and enjoy a round, either alone or with a partner if one could find one, and to take lessons from the pro. I gave a false name, of course, and paid always in cash. I was exactly the kind of interloper that no one took much notice of. Certainly no one evinced any desire to partner me. I would drink a solitary beer, have my lesson and quietly depart. The undersized, ordinary-looking, bespectacled boy had grown into an under-sized, ordinary-looking, bespectacled man. I had grown a moustache but there was otherwise little change. I had no fear that Manston-Green would recognise me but, taking no risks, I kept well out of his way.

And did I recognise Manston-Green when I first saw him after so many years? How could I fail to do so? He too was a grown-up version of the tormentor of my childhood. He was still tall but stout, carrying his stomach high, red-faced, loud-voiced, the black hair sleeked back. I could see that he was deferred to. He was the Wingco, Keith Manston-Green, prosperous businessman, provider of jobs and silver cups, slapper of backs, dispenser of free drinks.

And then I saw Shirley May, his second wife, drinking with her cronies at the bar. Shirley May. She was always called by that double first name, and behind her husband's back I occasionally caught their salacious whispers, 'Shirley May, but on the other hand, she may not!' He had got his trophy wife, blonde, though obviously not naturally so, voluptuous, long-legged, a second-hand film-star vision of feminine desirability. Even to look at her, standing at the club bar flirting with a group of bemused fools, made me sick.

It was then that I first began to see how I might kill her husband. And not only kill him, but make him suffer over months of protracted agony, just as he had made me suffer for years. The revenge wouldn't be perfect, but it would be as close as I could get.

The months I spent leading up to action had to be carefully planned. It was important that Manston-Green did not see me, or at least not close enough to recognise me, and that he never heard even my false name. That wasn't difficult. He played only at weekends and in the evenings, I chose Wednesday mornings. Even when our visits had coincided, the Wingco was far too important to cast his eyes on undistinguished temporary players only permitted on the greens because their fees were needed. It was important, too, that I didn't become even remotely interesting to other members. It was necessary to play badly, and on the few occasions that someone condescended to partner me, I played badly. That took some skill: I naturally have a very good eye. I had my story ready. I had an elderly and ailing mother living in the neighbourhood and was paying occasional dutiful visits. I embarked on boring descriptions of her symptoms and prognosis and would watch their eyes glazing over as they edged away. I kept my appearances infrequent; I did not want to become an object of gossip and curiosity even if both were dismissive. I needed to be too anonymous even to be regarded as the club bore.

Firstly, I needed a key to the clubhouse. For a locksmith that wasn't difficult. By careful watching I discovered that three people had keys, Manston-Green, the club secretary Bill Caraway, and the pro Alistair McFee. McFee's was the easiest to get my hands on. He kept it in the pocket of his jacket, which he invariably hung on the door of his office. I bided my time until one Wednesday morning, when he was occupied on the first green with a particularly demanding pupil, with gloved hands I took the key from his pocket and, locking myself in the lavatory, took an impression. On my next visit, surreptitiously, I tested the key. It worked.

I then began the second part of my campaign.

Late at night alone in my London office and wearing gloves, I cut out words from the national newspapers and pasted them onto a sheet of writing paper, the kind sold in every stationer's shop. The messages, which I sent twice weekly, had small variations of wording but always the same insinuating poison. Why did you marry that bitch? Don't you know she's having it off with someone else? Are you blind or something? Don't you know what Shirley May's up to? I don't like to see a decent man cheated. You should keep an eye on your wife.

Oh, they had their effect. On subsequent visits to the golf club when, carefully distanced, I watched them together I knew that my carefully calculated strategy was working. There were public quarrels. Members of the club began to edge away when they were together. The Wingco was rattled – and so, of course, was she.

I gave that marriage no more than two months. Which meant that I couldn't delay.

I fixed the actual date two weeks ahead. Only one other thing was necessary. I made sure that the new clubs I purchased were the same make as his, a necessary extravagance. I substituted my driver for his driver, handling it always with gloves. It was his prints I wanted, not mine. I made sure my final messages were received on the morning of the crucial day, his by post, hers pushed under the door when, watching, I saw him drive away for work. Hers said, If you want to know who's sending these notes, meet me in the clubhouse at nine tonight. Burn this note. A friend. His said the same, but gave a time ten minutes later.

I realised, of course, that neither might come. That was a risk I took. But if they didn't, I would be in no danger. It would simply mean that I needed to find another way of killing Manston-Green. I hoped it wouldn't be necessary. My plan was so perfect, the horror I had planned for him so wonderfully satisfying.

I won't distress you with details; they are not necessary. I had my keys to the clubhouse and I was waiting for her, her husband's driver in hand. As I said, I have a good eye. It took only two swings to kill her, three more to batter her face into a pulp. I dropped the driver, let myself out and locked the door. There was a public phone box at the end of the lane. When I asked for the police I was put through promptly and without trouble. I disguised my voice although it wasn't strictly necessary. It became the confused, high-pitched, terrified voice of an older man.

'I've just passed the golf club. There's screaming in the clubhouse. A woman. I think someone's killing her.' 'And your name and address, sir?' 'No, no. I'm not getting mixed up in this. It's nothing to do with me. I just thought I ought to let you know.' And with gloved hands I rang off.

They came, of course. They came just in time to see Manston-Green bending over his wife's body. I couldn't have planned that. I imagined they might have been late but would still have had the club with her blood and matted hair, the fingerprints, the evidence of quarrels. But they weren't late; they were just in time.

I resisted the temptation to go to the trial. It was irritating to have to forgo that pleasure, but I thought it prudent. Press photographs were being taken of the crowd, and although the chance of being recognised was infinitesimally small, why risk it? And I thought it sensible to continue going occasionally to the golf club, but less frequently. The talk was all of the murder, but no one bothered to include me. I took my solitary lessons and departed. He appealed, of course, and that was an anxious day for me. But the appeal failed and I knew that the end was now certain.

There were only three weeks between sentence and execution and they were probably the happiest of my life, not in the sense of an exultant joy, but of knowing myself at peace for the first time since I'd started at St Chad's. The week before the execution I was with him in spirit through every minute of every hour in that condemned cell. I knew what would happen on the morning when he would be launched out of this world and out of my mind. I pictured the arrival of the executioner the day before to fulfil Home Office requirements: the dropping of a sandbag in the presence of the governor to make sure that there would be no mishap and that the length of the drop was correct. I was with him as he peered through the spyhole in the door of the condemned cell, a cell only feet away from the execution chamber. It's a merciful death if not mishandled and I knew Manston-Green would die with less pain than probably would I. The suffering was in the preceding weeks and no one could truly experience that horror but he. In imagination I lived his last night, the restless turning and twisting, the strengthening light of the dreaded day, the breakfast he wouldn't be able to eat, the clumsy kindness of the constantly watching guards. I was with the hangman in imagination when he pinned Manston-Green's arms. I was part of that little procession which passed through the dreaded door, the white-faced governor of the prison present, the chaplain keeping his eyes on his prayer book held in shaking hands.

It's a quick death, only some twenty seconds from the moment the arms are pinioned to the drop itself. But there would be one moment when he would be able to see the scaffold, the noose hanging precisely at the level of his chest before the white hood was pulled into place. I exulted at the thought of those few seconds.

As usual I went to the prison the day before the execution. There were things to be done, instructions to be followed. I was greeted politely but I wasn't welcome.

I knew they felt contaminated when they shook my hand. And every prisoner in every cell knew that I was there. Already there was the expected din, shouting voices, utensils banged against the cell doors. A little crowd of protesters or morbid voyeurs was already collecting outside the prison gate. I am a meticulous craftsman, as was my father before me. I am highly experienced in my part-time job. And I think he knew me. Oh yes, he knew me. I saw the recognition in his eyes that second before I slipped the white hood over his head and pulled the lever. He dropped like a stone and the rope tautened and quivered. My life's task was at last accomplished and from now on I would be at peace. I had killed Keith Manston-Green.

MURDER MOST FOUL

'Death seems to provide the minds of the Anglo-Saxon race with a greater fund of innocent enjoyment than any other single subject.' So wrote Dorothy L. Sayers in 1934. She was, of course, thinking of murder; not the sordid, messy and occasionally pathetic murders of real life but the more elegantly contrived and mysterious concoctions of the detective novelist. To judge, too, from the universal popularity of the genre, it isn't only the Anglo-Saxons who share this enthusiasm for murder most foul. From Greenland to Japan, millions of readers are perfectly at home in Sherlock Holmes's claustrophobic sanctum at 221B Baker Street, Miss Marple's charming cottage at St. Mary Mead and Lord Peter Wimsey's elegant apartment in Piccadilly. There is nothing like a potent amalgam of mystery and mayhem to make the whole world kin.

When I came to write my first novel in the early sixties it never occurred to me to begin with anything but a mystery, partly I think because its highly disciplined form provides an admirable apprenticeship for a writer who aspires to become a serious novelist. I had always enjoyed the genre – Dorothy L. Sayers was a potent influence – and I was fascinated by the challenge of trying to do something new with the well-worn conventions of the detective story: the central mysterious death; the closed circle of suspects each with a credible motive; the arrival of the detective like the avenging deity of an old Morality Play; the final solution which the reader himself can arrive at by logical deduction from clues presented to him with deceptive cunning but essential fairness.

In my own reading it wasn't the puzzle which

most intrigued me and I sometimes think that fewer readers watch for every clue, note every twist in the plot and sniff happily after every red herring than we writers imagine. My younger daughter, reading my latest book, merely comments: 'It can't be him or her; you like them too much', and I suspect that most of us guess the murderer more through our knowledge of the author, their style, prejudices and foibles, than through close attention to every detail of the plot. We are pitting our wits primarily against the writer, not their villain or their detective.

So if correctly guessing the identity of the murderer isn't always the chief attraction, what is? Perhaps it is the age-old and universal pleasure provided by a well-told story with a beginning, a middle and an end, a tale which takes us into a world in which we know that wrong will finally be righted, the guilty exposed, the innocent vindicated, and human reason will triumph. Perhaps it is the frisson of vicarious terror and danger as we sit safely by our fireside or pull the bedclothes more comfortably under our chin. Above all, in our increasingly violent and irrational world – in which so many of our societal problems seem insoluble – the mystery offers the psychological comfort of a story, based on the premise that murder is still the unique crime, that even the most unpleasant character has the right to live to the last natural moment and that there is no problem, however difficult, which cannot be solved by human ingenuity, human intelligence and human courage. I suspect that these are some of the reasons why I enjoy mysteries. Perhaps they are also the reason why I choose to write them.

One of the ancillary pleasures of reading mysteries is that of discovering new facts and gaining an insight into different and fascinating worlds. It has been said that a good mystery consists of twenty-five per cent puzzle, twenty-five per cent characterisation and fifty per cent what the author knows best, and I, for one, have much enjoyed learning about horse racing from Dick Francis, theatrical life from Ngaio Marsh, banking from Emma Lathen and campanology from Dorothy L. Sayers. The setting, too, is of immense importance in transporting us to another world. I can gain a keener and more perceptive understanding of Californian life and mores from Ross Macdonald than from any travel book. I walk the bridges of Amsterdam with Nicolas Freeling's Van der Valk or swelter in the heat of Bombay with H. R. F. Keating's Inspector Ghote, while the very smells and sounds of Paris rise from the pages of Simenon.

At the risk of disappointing mystery fiends, I have to confess that I am not an addict in the sense that I have to have my daily fix even if the dose isn't up to strength or standard. My reading is discriminating and, I admit, somewhat limited. Much as I admire those fine writers Raymond Chandler and Dashiell Hammett (and their influences not only on crime writing but on the modern novel have been significant), I am not really an aficionado of the school of gun, guts and gore. I prefer a more domestic murder; the contrast between an ordered society or environment and the shocking and contaminating irruption of violent death. Those writers I most enjoy, Dorothy L. Sayers, Margery Allingham and Ngaio Marsh, are all experts in malice domestic and they conform to W. H. Auden's dictum that 'the corpse must shock not only because it is a corpse but also because, even for a corpse, it is shockingly out of place, as when a dog makes a mess on a drawing-room carpet'. All three worked within the conventions of the genre, yet all helped to raise the mystery from a subliterary puzzle to a form with serious claims to be regarded as a novel. All understood the importance of setting and atmosphere. All could create characters who are more than stereotypes waiting like cardboard cut-outs to be knocked down by the detective. All set their stories unambiguously in their time and place and made some attempt to combine the mystery with the novel of social realism. I would place Dorothy L. Sayers's *The Nine Tailors* high on my list of favourites while Margery Allingham's *Tiger in the Smoke* is probably among the best mysteries ever written. The opposing characters of the murderer, Jack Havoc, and the gentle but implacable

Canon Avril make nonsense of the criticism that the mystery is an essentially trivial form and that the great absolutes of good and evil are, and must always remain, outside its range.

It is interesting that all three writers are women as, of course, was that phenomenon, the Queen of Crime, Agatha Christie, a lady I think of less as a novelist than as a literary conjurer whose sleight of hand as she shuffles her cast of characters can outwit the keenest eye. Because this quartet of female experts in death is pre-eminent I am often asked the invidious question: 'Why are respectable middle-class ladies so good at murder?' It may be that literary mayhem is our way of sublimating our aggression or of purging irrational feelings of anxiety or guilt, but I doubt whether we need delve into psychological theory for an answer. The construction of clues demands a keen eye for the domestic details of everyday life, and in this women excel. Who was where and with whom and when? Who ate the poisoned salad and who prepared it? What woman would wear that purple lipstick found by the body? Who locked the library door and when? At what time precisely was that tell-tale red stain first noticed on the bedroom floor? And women are particularly skilled at dealing with the motives for murder, the tensions, intrigues, jealousies and resentments which can fester in the closed circles beloved of crime writers to erupt finally into the ultimate crime.

A bad mystery is the easiest of all books to write; a good mystery is among the most difficult. The problems of construction itself are formidable. So much has to be achieved within the eighty to ninety thousand words which are the average length for the genre. The characters of the detective, victim and up to half-a-dozen suspects must be firmly established and psychologically credible; the method of murder must be feasible and, if possible, original; the setting must both influence and enhance the mood of the story; the denouement – that most difficult chapter of all to write successfully – must be intellectually satisfying as well as exciting. The whole may be likened to one of those ingenious puzzles: oddly shaped pieces of wood which, when fitted together, form a perfect sphere. To achieve this, careful preliminary planning is essential before the first word is written. I usually make notes, not only of the weather, location and characters, but of where everyone is at the crucial time of death. I try to describe the murder realistically and I am sometimes asked whether I frighten myself. The answer has to be no. I can be frightened by the books of others, never by my own. Perhaps this is because, paradoxically, the writer needs to be both deeply involved in and yet detached from his work.

And what of the future? For years now critics have prophesied the demise of the mystery, at least in its traditional form. One nineteenth-century critic, reviewing Conan Doyle, wrote: 'In view of the difficulty of hitting on any fancies that are decently fresh, surely this sensational business must soon come to an end.' Certainly, it isn't easy to invent original ways of murder, while the exotic and sometimes bizarre settings of some modern mysteries bear witness to the almost desperate search for new locations and fresh ideas. 'Death hath a thousand doors to let out life' and most of them must have been used by now. Apart from the ubiquitous blunt instrument, shooting, hanging and throttling, the unfortunate victims have been despatched by the prolonged ringing of church bells; stabbing with an icicle; a bullet from a revolver triggered by the loud pedal of a piano; poison on the back of postage stamps; the injection of a bubble into a vein. A few have even been frightened to death.

But still the sensational business flourishes, a source of innocent relaxation, diversion and reassurance to new generations of readers. The modern mystery addict is, of course, more sophisticated than his counterpart in the heyday of the country-house murder when no cast was complete without the butler; when the library became established as the most lethal room in England; when the detective was invariably an amateur of impeccable lineage and superhuman talent while the professional police were bicycling buffoons deferentially tugging their forelocks to the gentry; and the denouement took place after dinner, with the whole cast in evening dress, when the least likely suspect would be unmasked as the murderer. Frequently he then obligingly killed himself to spare the readers the disagreeable thought of the public hangman.

The modern mystery has outgrown these naiveties and simplicities and those writers whose work will last are those who succeed in the difficult task of combining the old traditions of an exciting story and the satisfying exercise of rational deduction with the psychological subtleties and moral ambiguities of a good novel. Here, in the words of Robert Browning, we are indeed 'on the dangerous edge of things' where the writer is exploring that greatest of all mysteries, the human heart, and where there may be no neat and simple answer in the final chapter, not even for a Hercule Poirot or a Lord Peter Wimsey.

P. D. JAMES, 1982